Trucks on the Go

A Panorama Sticker Storybook

written by Mike Teitelbaum
illustrations by Thomas LaPadula

Pleasantville, New York • Montréal, Québec • Bath, United Kingdom

There's a new shopping center being built, and all kinds of trucks are needed to do all kinds of jobs. Workers are getting this site ready for construction. The loader scoops up rocks, then carries them over to the dump truck. The loader's big wheels roll right over the bumpy ground.

The loader dumps the rocks into the back of the dump truck. The back of the dump truck is called the bed. When the dump truck is full, it drives away.

The mighty bulldozer pushes big piles of soil and rocks. It smoothes out the ground so that building can begin.

When the ground is smooth and the rocks are gone, it's time for the backhoe to do its job. The backhoe has big tires with thick treads. This helps it move all around the construction site.

The backhoe has a metal claw attached to its mechanical arm. This claw is a big bucket with sharp teeth on the end. It's used for digging huge holes. The backhoe's claw reaches down and bites into the ground with its sharp teeth. Then it pulls forward and scoops the dirt into the bucket. The backhoe's mechanical arm lifts up the dirt and then dumps it in a pile.

Once the holes are dug, it's time to put the pipes in place. The crane is used to carry the pipes, then lower them into the holes. This crane moves along on special treads. These treads help the crane work in soft, muddy areas.

The crane has a long arm with a thick cable and hook connected to it. Other metal cables are placed in and around the pipes. Then the cables are attached to the crane's hook. Slowly the crane lifts the heavy pipes up, then lowers them into the hole. Now the building can begin!

The first step in putting up a building is creating a foundation. This is done by pouring wet concrete into wooden forms. The mixer is used to stir up the concrete to get it ready to pour. A big, round metal container, called a drum, sits on the back of the mixer.

The drum is filled with sand, gravel, cement, and water—the ingredients for making concrete. The mixer's drum then spins around and around until the concrete is ready. Then the concrete pours out of the drum, down a chute, and into the forms. When the concrete dries, it becomes hard. Then the wooden forms can be removed. The foundation walls are ready.

It's time to use the crane again. This time, the crane has a bucket attached to its arm. The crane lowers the bucket using a thick cable. The bucket opens wide and scoops up a load of gravel.

Once the gravel is inside the bucket, the crane turns its long arm. When the bucket is above the dump truck, it opens up again, dumping the gravel into the bed of the dump truck. Then the crane swings back toward the pile of gravel to scoop up another bucketful.

Things are really moving now at the construction site. The dump truck delivers a load of gravel. When it arrives, the dump truck raises its bed and dumps the gravel just where the workers need it. Next, the gravel is spread over the dirt. When the gravel is all spread, the steamroller is ready to go to work.

The steamroller is very, very heavy! That's how it does its job. Its huge, heavy roller presses down the gravel as it rolls. This helps build a strong base for the roads and sidewalks that will go on top of the gravel. The bulldozer continues to clear away rocks and dirt, and smooth out the ground.

The gravel is pressed down to create a base. Sidewalks have been poured from concrete. The foundations are dry. Now it's time to build the buildings. The construction workers will need bricks, cinder blocks, wood, and windows. All of these items arrive on the forklift.

The forklift is used to carry heavy loads on wooden boards called pallets. The forklift has two long metal arms that stick out in front. These arms slide under the wooden pallets. Then the arms lift up, taking the bricks or other building material with them. The forklift has big thick tires. It rolls along carrying a heavy load. But it's small enough to deliver the load right where it's needed.

Finally, the construction is done. The buildings are complete. The roads and sidewalks are finished. A stone fountain has been built. For the final touch, the crane lowers a brand new sign into place. The shopping center will soon be ready to open, thanks to all the mighty trucks on the go!